Wanted — 7 Fearless Engineers!

By

Warner Van Lorne

Wanted — 7 Fearless Engineers!

by Warner Van Lorne

ISBN: 978-93-57279-59-8

Published by

DOUBLE 9 BOOKS

2/13-B, Ansari Road
Daryaganj, New Delhi – 110002
info@double9books.com
www.double9books.com
Tel. 011-40042856

ABOUT THE AUTHOR

Editor of the influential Astounding Stories and other science fiction magazines, Frederick Orlin Tremaine was an American (born January 7, 1899—died October 22, 1956). He oversaw a variety of publishing enterprises, edited a number of other periodicals, and occasionally wrote fiction. In the spring of 1920, when Tremaine was a junior at Valparaiso, he served as the news editor of the Torch, the weekly student newspaper. He held the position of Editor-in-Chief from 1920 to 1921, his senior year. After graduating, he took a position on the staff of a newspaper in New York City. He worked as an associate editor at The Eastern Underwriter in NYC toward the end of 1922. He then went on to the Macfadden magazine group. He served as Macfadden's Brain Power and Beautiful Womanhood's managing editor in May 1923. On June 1, 1923, he was appointed editor of the esteemed Metropolitan Magazine, which was later renamed Macfadden Fiction-Magazine Lovers for the issue published in October 1924. He took over as editor of the main publication True Story Magazine at the start of 1924. He also claimed to have designed the first issues of True Detective, True Experiences, and True Romances.

CONTENTS

CHAPTER I.
Opportunity 7

CHAPTER II.
Out to Sea 14

CHAPTER III.
Strange Destination 22

CHAPTER IV.
Morquil's Story 27

CHAPTER V.
Voyaging to Another World 33

CHAPTER VI.
An Engineer's Mettle 39

CHAPTER VII.
Jupiter and Trouble! 46

CHAPTER VIII.
Battle with a Monster 53

A great civilization's fate lay in Dick Barrow's hands as he led his courageous fellow engineers into a strange and unknown land. None of them knew what lay ahead—what dangers awaited them—or what rewards. But they did not hesitate because the first question asked them had been: "Are you a brave man?"

CHAPTER I.

Opportunity

FROM where Dick Barrow sat, hundreds of men were visible, occupying benches in every manner of position. Some stretched at full length, sleeping in the morning sun after a night in the park. Others sat with heads hanging; thinking thoughts of their own.

Depression or recession, it meant the same to all of them. Some didn't care, but others tried to find any kind of work that would fill their stomachs with food.

For three days Dick hadn't eaten a good meal, and felt almost as low as the derelicts whom he had for companions. He would have enjoyed a smoke, but turned away as two men dove for a cigarette-butt; discarded by a passerby.

Anyone who could afford to buy a newspaper was an aristocrat, and Dick watched until he saw one discarded. For three days he had been reading them secondhand, but the only jobs were too far to walk and apply for.

His eyes stopped at one item in the column and a puzzled frown slowly puckered his forehead.

> Wanted: An Engineer. Young man with love for electrical and mechanical work, who is not afraid of isolation. Have some knowledge of engineering, but general experience more desirable than specialized training. Must be willing to leave country, never to return; for which he will be well remunerated. Have no close family ties, and willing to submit to certain amount of danger. Will be isolated with few members of own race, but will have great opportunity to develop mastery of huge machines. Come prepared to leave for post immediately, without preparation. Every want will be taken care of by employers. This position is for lifetime, without opportunity of turning back after having accepted responsibility. GREAT OPPORTUNITY! Room 36, 18 W. Morgan Ave., City.

For a long time Dick Barrow gazed at the ad, mentally comparing his own qualifications for the position—and they *seemed* to fit! He was not a graduate engineer, being forced to quit school after two years of study. Three years later his father died, then Dick lost the job that had kept them eating regularly. His love of mechanics remained insatiable, and he constantly hoped for work which would allow him to use his knowledge and ability.

He had no relations, and the *only* girl had forgotten him, when he left school. He heard that she married a classmate!

Dick was twenty-seven. Five years had slipped by since he quit school, and he couldn't remember where they had gone. It was only six months after his father died that he lost his last regular job. He tried selling and was a failure. He had been carpenter's helper, plumber's helper, porter, counter-man and busboy as the months passed, but nothing steady. For the past two months he had been hunting for work, while his few dollars dwindled to where he no longer had room rent. Then it was the park.

His feet were sore and blistered from holes in his shoes, and he limped with every step. It took so long to reach the address that there was little chance of finding the job still open. It was not the first time he had missed—for the same reason.

He found that 18 Morgan Avenue was a dreary structure, appearing as if it had been standing twenty years too long. The wooden stairs creaked as he rested his weight on first one sore foot and then the other. Room 36 was at the top of the five-story building, and it seemed ages before he reached the doorway. The only sign of furnishing in the room was a hard bench, occupied by three men. Dick had to stand while his feet tortured him, but it was hopeful to see men waiting—*the job wasn't filled*!

Suddenly a door at the opposite side of the room jerked open and a man dashed through.

"Get out of here! The man's *insane*!"

Two of the men followed, but the man who remained on the bench glanced at Dick, grinned, shrugged his shoulders and entered the door. A moment later his booming voice could be heard through the thin partition, although his words were not clear.

An hour passed while Dick waited. When the man came out, with a smile on his face, he wished Dick luck and headed for the stairway.

Barrow felt a queer sensation as he stepped through the inner doorway. A man faced him in a huge leather chair across the room. At least Dick thought he was a man. Grotesque in every way, his body was small while his head was twice as large as normal. He was light complexioned, with almost white hair thinly covering the top of his enormous head. His features were finely cut, with large aquiline nose. He was not repulsive, and smiled in welcome as Dick hesitated at the threshold. When he spoke his tone was soft and musical.

"Welcome, stranger. You have come in answer to my advertisement and I will explain without wasting time. But first tell me about yourself."

Going over his complete life history, including the two years in college, Dick came to the lean years when his father died. He hesitated slightly not proud of this period.

"Go on, Mr. Barrow. It is not important to have been a success in business, and I will not consider that in your applications. It isn't what you *have* done, but what you *want* to do, that interests me."

He spoke with a strange accent, that Dick didn't recognize. But he was pleasant and made it easy to talk.

When Barrow finished, by relating the finding of the newspaper and the long walk to the office, the queer man was smiling.

"I like your frankness and will tell you about the position, although I can't reveal the location of your work. It is not on any map, and you will work among a race such as myself, with no opportunity of leaving after reaching the destination.

"You will be given every comfort and advantage among my people, and be required to work hard in return. There are several machines out of commission which must be repaired and put to work again. After a few months your work will be easier, although you must constantly watch all machinery to see that it is in perfect condition, and does not stop work for even a moment.

"My people use mechanics of greater size and development than anything you have ever seen, and our lives depend on its perfect operation. In order to accept this position you must be married. Your wife must come with you, and be willing to accept the same living conditions which are offered to you.

"The man who left this office as you entered has a fiancee and has gone to talk it over with her. In your instance *I must select your wife*! You will be the leader of the workmen whom I take back. There will be only a few people such as yourself, and you can never again see others of your race.

"You will have power and wealth among my people, and every type of entertainment that you desire. But remember that you leave your race forever, with *no possibility* of return! If you accept my offer you must trust entirely in what I say about the future."

When the man finished speaking Dick was quiet for a long time. Everything seemed so unreal, so different from what he had expected. He must be willing to leave everything that he had always known—to enter an existence which he didn't understand—without chance of return! Yet he believed every word this man spoke, impossible as it seemed. But *marriage* ... with a girl he had never *seen*!

The man spoke again. "You hesitate about marrying; I can see it in your eyes. But remember that *she* must accept without knowing you, and is taking just as great a chance. This I can say. She will be brilliant, and I *could not* trust you to pick out a brilliant woman for your wife. Love would come first in your eyes. Other things would seem unimportant. I know that you and the girl I select are apt to fall in love, as I shall choose a girl suitable to your temperament."

Dick answered slowly, "I don't know what to say. I will have to live with her all of my life, and if we are not happy anything you could offer would mean nothing."

The smile spread over the strange man's face again. "I wouldn't worry too much. I believe you could stand a greater chance of happiness if *I* do the choosing than if you do it yourself as I can see more of the future. If you are mutually likable and willing to understand each other; if you are mentally on the same level, there is little chance of *not* falling in love. My race mates in this way, and it works out better than your haphazard mating."

When he realized that Dick still hesitated, he was slightly upset. Then reaching into a leather bag, hung from a strap around his neck, he stretched forth a handful of bills.

"Go and get yourself a good meal. It is now morning. When two more mornings have passed come again. Don't be afraid to use the money for anything that you desire. This does not mean that I expect you to accept the offer, but it will allow you to think it over carefully—without thinking of your *stomach*. Buy clothes, a room to sleep in, anything else that you want. Be comfortable and do not worry about what you spend. If you refuse my terms, I will be disappointed, but will not expect to be repaid."

As Dick reached the street he shook his head. It all seemed so fantastic. But the money in his hand was real money—and there was a lot of it! Suddenly he realized that people were staring at the handful of bills, and he hurriedly stuffed them in a pocket. When he was alone for a moment he stepped into a vacant doorway to count it.

There were 14 twenties, 10 fifties, and three ten dollar bills in the lot. Twenty-seven bills in all, representing eight hundred and ten dollars. Folding the money carefully and placing it in a safe pocket, he noticed a sign across the street. "SHOES," it said. He glanced at his own, then limped slowly across when the traffic lights changed. For a moment he looked in the window, then stepped inside.

While the shoe clerk was busy he carefully slipped a twenty from the other bills. It would seem strange if he had too much money with his feet in such shape.

The next stop was a restaurant. Then followed a trip to a clothing store—and he left his old suit behind. With new clothes, shoes, and a meal beneath his belt, he began to think the offer of the stranger was far from fantastic. What if he did have to marry a strange girl? At least they would both have comfort and companionship, wherever they went.

Barrow's first appointment was on Tuesday morning, and Friday found him climbing the same stairs. He watched the papers but there had been no repetition of the advertisement. Evidently the strange man had all the applicants he wanted.

The outer office was empty, but when he opened the inner door, the queer man was smiling just as Dick remembered him.

"Come in, Mr. Barrow. I'm glad to see you. I was surprised to hear of your use of the money, but was pleased rather than disappointed. You did well."

For a moment Dick was taken back, then he smiled sheepishly. "I don't know just what to say, Sir, I did so many things. But I didn't know I was being watched."

"Every move you made was watched carefully, and reported to me. I know where you spent every hour since you left here the other morning. I wanted to know how you would act with money enough to do as you pleased for a few days. You acted wisely, and I'm glad that you spent so much of it on men who need it. You bought twenty-two pairs of shoes, thirty-six shirts and forty-five suits of underwear. You also bought cheap suits for nine men and several odd and end accessories as well.

"Out of the total sum you spent less than one hundred dollars for yourself, and yet you have only forty-two dollars of the sum I handed you. The remainder you used for meals and cheap lodging for the men you have taken care of in the past three days. You have gone through a lot of money since you were here."

Dick stammered as he spoke, "I'm sorry, sir, but I thought—"

"You thought *just right*! I *did* give you the money to use as you pleased and I'm proud of the way you spent it. But I want to know the answer. You must have decided by this time. If the answer is yes, you will bind yourself to a lifetime of work. If it is no, we will say goodbye."

Dick's face lighted with a smile. "The answer is *yes*. I am proud to leave my future in your hands—even to my marriage. I made up my mind to do as you desire, and am prepared to leave any time you are ready. I hope you have hired every one you need and that we will all enjoy our new work."

"You're a brave man, Dick Barrow." There was admiration in the voice of the stranger. "If you remained here I believe you would make your mark in life, but you will have even greater opportunity where you are going. I believe your decision will prove to be a happy one.

"You must stay at a good hotel. Reasonable if you want, although it is not important. I will send the girl to you within a few days. You will be married as soon as possible after you meet her.

"She will bring a letter and will do exactly as you say. I will allow time for you to get acquainted before I have further orders. From that time you will obey my orders explicitly and follow every instruction without question. Every member of the party will take orders from you, and *you must give them*!"

Once more Dick was handed a handful of bills as he prepared to leave, and knew there was even more than the first time. But he would live in constant dread of meeting the girl he was to marry. As he started to open the door, the man spoke again.

"Use the money as you desire. It will be your last chance of spending any and I want you to enjoy yourself as much as possible during the time remaining. Do what you like for the men in the park or any others you wish to help. If you need more money send a messenger to this room, but don't come yourself. Don't contact me again until my orders require it. Have a good time."

Dick felt that he was living a dream, but a very pleasant one. Just one thought disturbed him. Who the girl would be—and what she would be like?

CHAPTER II.

Out to Sea

THE following morning an advertisement appeared in the papers, under the heading of help wanted: woman. It was the same address on Morgan Avenue. His heart sank! The man was *advertising* for a wife! Now Barrow *knew* he was in for a tough streak of luck. He read it carefully.

> Opportunity for young lady. Must be of age, single, brilliant, with good family background. Higher education not necessary. Must be willing to travel long distance. Must not be averse to marriage with brilliant young man; give up all former associations, with no possibility of return; live life in small community of own race, with no possibility of communication with former home. Must be without close family ties, or relationship. Opportunity to live life of luxury and ease, with amiable group far from present home and civilization. Young lady who fits qualifications will not regret applying for position. Honor, love and security will be her reward. OPPORTUNITY! Room 36, 18 West Morgan Avenue, City.

While Dick was eating dinner on Tuesday evening, a young lady fell headlong in front of his table. A moment later she was seated in the chair opposite his own. Ten minutes later he was ordering her dinner.

Afterward, as they walked toward a movie, Dick felt as if he was committing a crime. He was supposed to meet his future wife—and instead was entertaining this young lady who had fallen into his life. When he learned that she was staying at the same hotel, they made a date for breakfast the next morning.

Dolores Dunbar was good company, and seemed willing to spend most of her time in Dick's company. He learned that she was as friendless as himself, and wondered why they couldn't have met before he made the strange bargain. But as the third day drew to a close she appeared apprehensive.

When she kept glancing around, as if expecting someone, Dick became curious, and felt rather hurt to think she was looking for someone else. Finally she spoke.

"I'm sorry, Dick, that I've made use of you the way I have, but I was ordered to do it. You see, my employer told me to meet you and spend every possible moment in your company. He also said that I would become acquainted with someone through you, and that you would know who he was, when I said I came from the large-headed man on Morgan Avenue—with a letter."

For a moment Dick was stunned. Then he laughed, a sickly, half-hearted laugh. When he found his voice it squeaked.

"I think we had better go to my room. We have some very private things to say."

The queer man had succeeded in their being together for three days before either knew *they* were the central figures in the drama. Now they felt farther apart than at any moment since they had met, but nervously admitted they had fared better than they expected.

They were married in the morning, to keep the agreement, but didn't consider it part of the bargain to live as man and wife.

Dick found only one order in the letter, to be at the office at ten o'clock on Tuesday morning. That left five days to enjoy themselves.

In spite of the stiffness between them Dick noticed how the light caught in Dolores' dark hair, and how her brown eyes sparkled at each new sight. Her head reached just above his shoulder, and he had never danced with a better partner. She enjoyed his company, and admitted to herself that he was a perfect gentleman.

During the five days they saw every good show, and visited every popular night club. Things they had always wanted to do were packed into the short time to themselves. Dick hired a car, and they drove for hours through the country. When Tuesday morning came they were tired, and it was hard to get up in time to keep the appointment.

When they opened the door, the big-headed man laughed at their yawns. "I see that you've either *been* enjoying yourselves, or have been *trying* mighty hard. You can make up your sleep from now on, as it will be a long time before we reach our destination. How do you like each other for permanent companions?"

Their faces grew crimson. Finally Dick found his voice. "I'm perfectly satisfied, Sir. I think Dolores is very pretty, and is *very* good company!"

He looked the other way to hide his embarrassment, as the girl spoke.

"I feel the same way. We have enjoyed being together, and perhaps when we are better acquainted the stiffness will disappear. We both feel odd, because we were required to marry!"

The strange man laughed out loud at this. "In other words you *might* have fallen in love, if you had been allowed time to do it. But *having* to marry creates an entirely different feeling. I believe it will work out well, even though you feel cheated at the moment. But we haven't any time to lose. Everyone is at the dock and we sail in two hours.

"Here are your instructions, Dick. From now on *you* give the orders, and I remain in the background. They will all feel more comfortable under the command of one of their own race. Study everything carefully on the way to the dock, then give them as your own orders."

Dick had little time for anything except to look through the sheaf of papers. On one sheet was a list of seven couples, with stateroom numbers beside each. His own was on the top, with number three room. This he dropped in a side pocket where it would be easy to find. The remainder was in connection with sailing.

Dick, Dolores and the big-headed man occupied one cab, while the baggage followed in another. Dolores had obtained quite a wardrobe, much to the amusement of her employer. But the man spoke only once during the trip.

"Everyone in the party must consider that they work for you, Dick. You must hear all complaints and settle all differences. They must not approach me for any reason. I am known as Morquil, of section one, which you will understand when we reach our destination."

The crew was hurrying back and forth on the deck of the small ship, taking care of last-minute details. A group of people were gathered beside a huge stack of baggage, and Dick walked toward them without waiting for the others.

Dolores went up the gangplank beside Morquil, helping him slightly. He seemed to have difficulty in supporting his enormous head with the slight body.

As Dick reached the group, he read the names from the list in his hand. "Mr. and Mrs. John McCarthy. You are in stateroom number seven. Take what baggage you can carry, the rest will be put on board." He called each name and stateroom; they headed for the ship. John McCarthy he found was the man he had met in the office, and he *still* had his perpetual grin. Evidently his fiancee had agreed to the pact for they were now man and wife.

When Dick started toward the ship, after watching the baggage put on board, he was stopped by a tap on the shoulder. The cab drivers were still waiting for their money. Morquil had left everything in his hands, even to paying for the motor trip to the dock.

It was a strange departure, with only a few people on the dock to say goodbye. Even they were just neighbors of the passengers. Most of the women on board were crying as the *Primrose* nosed out through the harbor toward the open sea.

Dick was still at the rail when the captain approached. "I'm sorry to bother you, Mr. Barrow, but I must know our destination so I can set the course."

The young leader's day dreaming was cut short, to jerk him back to his duties. He felt that the lives and hopes of everyone on the ship had been thrust into his hands.

Even the captain didn't know where they were going. The ship had been chartered for a voyage of several months, to an unknown destination. He and the crew were well paid, and didn't care where they went.

Dick drew a sealed envelope from his pocket, detached a slip of paper and handed it to the captain. He read the note, then repeated it.

"You are to keep the destination to yourself. No one on the ship is to know where we are going, and you will not mention it to me again. I hope that we have good weather, Captain, and a fast trip."

Barrow felt like a fool. Repeating messages as if they were his own—without the slightest knowledge of what they were about. *He* was supposedly charting the course—and didn't have the slightest idea where they were going.

When Dick reached his stateroom (after answering questions from everyone on board—and telling them nothing) he found Dolores sobbing. She had kept her smile until the boat sailed. Now she was crying her eyes out. It was not a new sight, as every woman on the ship seemed occupied in the same way, with the men trying to comfort them.

As Dick sat down beside her, he could feel the throb of the diesel motor. It seemed to carry the rhythm of adventure through the walls of the cabin, giving the feeling of the unknown. For a long time there was silence while Dolores held one of Dick's hands for protection.

"Dick! We only have *one* cabin! I'm supposed to stay here with you—and I *hardly know you*! Morquil told me that I must stay here, there are no extra rooms."

"I'm sorry, Dolores. We will just have to put up with things as they are. We've got into this and will have to see it through. After all, we *are* man and wife, and the people on board would think it strange if we didn't occupy the same room. There are two bunks, so I won't have to sleep on the floor. It will be a long trip, and we might as well enjoy it as much as possible."

Days changed into weeks as the ship plowed steadily south. They stopped at one port for a few hours to refuel, but there was little to see. The ship was slow and it felt good to walk on land again. But no one spoke enough English to answer questions.

It was the only time they sighted land until just before the end of the trip, when small islands began to slide by. Some within a few hundred feet, others just visible in the distance. Morquil hadn't appeared on deck during the entire trip, but now he approached the rail.

His face lighted with an ethereal glow as he gazed across the blue water. He looked like a man who was sighting his home after many years of absence. Dick couldn't help but feel glad for him, while cold chills of misgiving crept up and down his own spine. Their voyage was ending at a far different place that he had pictured in his mind, and quite the opposite of the description which Morquil had given of gigantic mechanical development.

They were passing by small south-sea islands, where mechanical equipment was out of the question. They hardly appeared *habitable*!

When the captain approached Dick, Morquil joined the conversation. "*I'll* give you the directions, Captain. Mr. Barrow is not feeling well, and I can do it for him.

"In about an hour we will reach the island, and I will point out the entrance to the harbor. It is well protected and there is no need to worry about any storm while we unload."

Every inch of space in the ship was packed with supplies. There were crates of books as well as pieces of machinery. Considerable radio equipment included assembled sets as well as parts. There were rifles and even one small cannon. Several crates of chickens and turkeys joined the other things on the beach. Then to the amazement of the party, a crate of pigs appeared.

It required three days to empty the ship, and with each passing hour the little party grew more apprehensive. It seemed as if they had been transferred to an island to start a *new* civilization, instead of a place where mechanical development was far advanced. Because Dick was the leader of the party, the others began to look at him with hatred; Morquil was almost forgotten.

When the last piece of equipment was covered with heavy tarpaulins, they constructed a shelter against one side of the pile. It was almost dark when everything was finished, and the captain decided to wait until the next day to sail. Everyone was invited on board the *Primrose*, for a farewell party.

Dick was forced to call a meeting in the main cabin, to forestall danger of the party deserting with the ship. Morquil had instructed him carefully.

"Friends, we are facing a great adventure. I'm in no different position than you, except that as leader I am responsible for whatever happens. I must take all blame for whatever comes, yet know that it will eventually work out as we expected.

"You all know that it is forbidden to talk about this trip, or to surmise our destination. I can assure you that it is done for your benefit, and later you will appreciate the fact that you did *not* know the future. I can't say what the next few days will bring to all of us, but be assured that everything you have been promised will be fulfilled.

"At the moment it seems impossible that things can turn out as we expected, but they *will*! You must simply be patient, and do not lose faith in this great adventure."

As Dick finished his speech, Morquil smiled, well satisfied. Dolores even smiled faintly, although it required effort to overcome her feeling of disaster.

The following morning everyone went ashore, and John McCarthy went around trying to aid Barrow in cheering up the party. He lied like a trooper, whispering to everyone that he had discovered something that satisfied *him* about the marvelous civilization they would reach before long.

Word of this reached Morquil, and he hurriedly called Dick and John out of sound of the others. He appeared almost frightened, and the moment they were alone, he spoke.

"What have you learned? I wanted you to know nothing, and it is better if you are ignorant. Whatever you learned is too much, and may upset the future."

John started to laugh, then seeing the expression of agony on the face of Morquil, he stopped short. "Don't worry. I haven't learned *anything*! I simply tried to help Dick keep the people satisfied. They were getting so restless they *needed* something. In my home town I was known as a famous liar, and thought my ability might come in handy."

Slowly the agony disappeared from Morquil's face. "Someday you will understand how much you have done for me, John. You will never regret it!"

The McCarthys remained jovial, and tried to keep up the spirits of the others as the days of loneliness passed.

Philip Jones and his wife were quiet, and waited patiently. Andrew and Emma Smith had taken over the cooking, and served the meals. George and Mary Martin were the youngest couple, and

Dick doubted whether either of them was past twenty-one. The others were all nearer thirty. They spent their time side by side, gazing over the sea, perfectly happy in each other's company.

Jerold Brown and Peter Yarbro were constantly fishing, from the collapsible boat, while their wives played cards.

One night they were awakened by brilliant flashes of light. Running to the beach, they watched in amazement.

They appeared like big guns firing just above the surface of the water, a few miles away. While they watched they gradually faded out. It was like a terrific electric storm, and the little party drew close together for comfort.

When the lights faded out entirely, Morquil told them to get some sleep. They would have to move equipment aboard a new ship the following day.

With the first streak of dawn Dick was back at the edge of the beach, straining his eyes into the gloom, but it was almost an hour before any object was visible.

After breakfast the ship was much plainer. They could see a rounded hull, like the top of a huge submarine, above the water. One of the women remarked that she would *stay* on the island before she'd enter an undersea ship. The trip on the *Primrose* was bad enough, but it wasn't *below* the surface.

Morquil called them within the canvas shelter, as if to make a speech. He held a small ball in one hand, and while they waited for instructions it landed in their midst.

A cloud of yellow vapor burst from the object, and everyone in the party slowly sank to the ground. Morquil joined the others in unconscious stupor, a victim of his own gas.

CHAPTER III.

Strange Destination

WHEN Dick opened his eyes, there was a feeling of motion to the bed. The strangeness of the ceiling overhead drew his attention. It was not canvas, but shiny metal, almost purple in tint.

Suddenly he sat up. Dolores lay beside him. As his eyes cleared of the lingering mist, objects in the room became plainer. They were in a luxuriously equipped cabin.

Dolores slowly opened her eyes. A moment later she sat up beside him. Glancing through the porthole, beyond the bed, she turned away with a groan.

"We *are* under water! And deep! I can't see a thing but strange blue light."

When Dick joined her, his forehead puckered in a frown. "No, Dolores. It doesn't look like water, it looks more like—No! *It can't be!*"

For several minutes there was silence while he gazed through the opening. Dolores had lost interest in the outside and was examining the fittings of the cabin. It had everything that could be desired in a first class hotel room, and many little toilet articles besides.

Suddenly Dick turned away. "*It's true!* We're in the air—*or above it*! Dolores, this ship is an *aircraft*!"

"Never mind, Dick, this room is *beautiful*! Whether we're flying or swimming, this is the nicest room I ever had. It has *everything*, and *look* at the dressing table!"

Dick sat down in amazement, a smile slowly spreading over his face. Dolores was happy—wherever they were. The room was all that mattered. But he couldn't understand why Morquil had gassed them, and put them on board unconscious. *He* would have enjoyed seeing the new ship.

When a knock sounded at the door, Dolores was unpacking her clothes for the first time since they left the *Primrose*. Turning the knob, Morquil stepped in.

"I'm sorry, Dick, that I had to use gas, but I knew the people would be afraid of boarding this ship. John McCarthy is down in the power room already, examining the machines, but some of the others are upset about the transfer from the island. I hope you don't feel resentful?"

"No, Morquil. We're satisfied. If you don't believe it—look at Dolores. She decided to like this room the minute she saw it, and is unpacking already."

The worried expression disappeared from the strange man's face. "I had the cabins equipped for women, as I know they are particular about such things."

"Would you like to see the ship? It will be your home for a long time, and you might as well get acquainted. I'm sorry that no one but myself understands English, but you will have ample time to learn our language during the voyage. You must speak it fluently by the time we arrive."

As they started out, Dolores dropped the dress she was holding, to join them. Curiosity overcame the desire to straighten out her clothes.

Entering a wide passage, they turned to the right. It ended abruptly in a room with several comfortable chairs. Three tables occupied the center in uneven positions, the underparts filled with metal-covered books. Two men of Morquil's race looked up at their approach.

Dick returned their friendly smile. When Dolores smiled they appeared embarrassed; but truly greatly pleased. Barrow noticed that one of them was examining a book in English; the illustrations seemed to fascinate him.

A narrow passage, beyond the main cabin, led to the control room where three men sat in swivel chairs. The instrument board was a marvel to Dick, and he watched for several minutes. It would require months to understand even a small portion of the gauges.

The ship was built with two decks, and a large hold beneath the lower floor which contained the machinery. The strange men were quartered on the lower level, with the exception of Morquil. His cabin was next to the one occupied by the Barrows. The McCarthys were on the opposite side of the passage, in a room slightly smaller than the one allotted to Dick and his wife.

The quarters of the remainder of the party were smaller, but still quite comfortable; all located farther back on the same passage.

Morquil was proud of the ship, and displayed each section with pride. He opened every cupboard door, and showed them through all of the cabins. They were stopped for a while, when they met Mrs. Yarbro, trying to dispel her fear of the strange craft. The others appeared to be taking their new quarters for granted, and settling down for the trip.

The main cabin was toward the front of the ship, while the dining room was at the rear; the staterooms on the passage between. One stairway led to the lower level, from just back of the control room, another from the dining saloon. A ramp beneath the rear stairway led to the hold of the ship. When they started down, Dolores returned to her cabin. Her interest ended on the upper decks.

Dick spotted John, bending over one of the machines, so engrossed that he didn't hear their approach. One of the crew stood nearby, watching.

When McCarthy saw Barrow, he nearly burst with enthusiasm. "This is the greatest thing I've ever seen! Why, it almost *talks*! Do you know, this little machine actually picks up the orders from the control room, and *adjusts every machine down here*! Darned if I don't think it's got a brain!"

When Morquil led the way toward the front of the hold, John was still engrossed in the apparatus. "He will be a valuable man to you, Dick, and can solve many problems that you would otherwise have to do yourself. He will make an able assistant."

Passing by the heavy machinery, they approached an enclosed section, which appeared to be of recent installation. Stepping through the doorway, Morquil threw a switch which lighted every corner, then watched expectantly as Dick examined the strange objects. It appeared to be a colony of metal beehives, with covered passages between.

"It is our home, Dick. This room contains everything in miniature that you will see when we arrive. Each of the smaller domes house thirty thousand people, the large one three times that number. We are born, live our lives, and die beneath these metal ceilings. It will be your job to care for them.

"Everything beneath these domes is exactly as it is in our cities, except that the machines are dummies. This model room was installed so you could study our civilization during the trip. When you arrive you will be ready to start work.

"You, and you only will have a key. You may bring any member of your party here that you desire, but it is not necessary for them to understand the entire civilization. There are only six cities, including the large one, where you and John McCarthy will be located. The other men will each have one dome under their control.

"It is easy to travel back and forth, and you may gather together at any time, although each of you will have duties in different sections. While you are overseeing the work in the smaller cities John can look after the capital. Upon your arrival in Yorpun you will take complete charge of all mechanical work. It will be your responsibility from then on."

As Dick slipped the key in his pocket, he felt the weight of a country settle slowly on his shoulders. Two hundred and ten thousand people—entirely dependent upon *his* control of the machines.

Where could this settlement be? They had sailed darn near to the end of the world in the *Primrose,* and now they were going even farther. From the way the metal domes covered the cities, it might be at the south pole, and still be habitable.

By the time they returned to the main cabin, it was dinner time. It was past mid-day when he regained consciousness, and Dick was hungry.

Mrs. McCarthy was knitting a sweater for her husband, while three of the strange men watched in amazement. Her knitting needles seemed to hold them spellbound. The other members of Dick's party were sitting around trying to decide what to do. But the sound of the dinner gong, made them forget their worries.

Dick had to go down to the hold and call John, who was still watching the master machine. If he hadn't been dragged away, he would have spent the night examining the strange device.

The meal was simple, but they all enjoyed it. It seemed to dispel the gloom from the party, and they appreciated McCarthy's jokes. There were fifteen of Morquil's race in the crew, and all but the men at the controls joined them.

Knives and forks stood at the places set for the passengers, brought from the supplies on the *Primrose,* but the crew ate with long narrow spoons. Table silver was evidently unknown to this race of people.

After dinner Morquil called them to the main cabin, and for the first time told about the destination. All that had kept them from losing hope long before, was his promise of greater comfort and luxury than they could hope for in their native land.

"I know that some of you resent the fact that you were unconscious while put aboard this ship. But I know you would hesitate to come of your own accord. One woman said that she wouldn't go on an *undersea* ship, and she would be more afraid of this.

"You will be amazed to know that we are now leaving the atmosphere of the earth that you have always known. *Our destination is on a different planet!"*

CHAPTER IV.

Morquil's Story

FOR a long time there was silence, then Mrs. Jones fainted. McCarthy took it without flinching, and his wife was satisfied if he was. Dick had suspected something almost as strange, and did not seem surprised. Dolores looked at him for guidance. He nodded reassuringly. The others shut their lips tight, feeling that they had been taken prisoner without hope of escape.

After a pause, Morquil continued. Mrs. Jones had recovered her composure and was staring at him with undisguised dislike. "I'm sorry it had to happen this way, but I would not have been able to take sufficient people if you had known where we were going. Some of you might have come, but I treated every one alike.

"I also was unconscious from the gas, but the crew revived me. I had to look after the loading of the supplies, and have the cabins prepared for you. It was much nicer that way than if you had resisted, and were put on board by force.

"I shall start at the beginning of my story, and let you judge for yourselves as to whether we have done wrong.

"The existence of my world depends on the perfect operation of machines. Even our atmosphere is manufactured and kept at proper temperature within sealed domes, to protect us from the natural gases of the planet. We live on this planet through necessity—*not desire*!

"Our race landed there very long ago after escaping from a planet that was falling into the sun. Their space ship ran short of fuel within the gravity pull of our present habitation. It was difficult, but they succeeded in constructing gas-proof shelters, and slowly improved conditions for living.

"We never knew what happened to the other space ships from our original planet, but they may be distributed throughout the universe. Your *own* ancestors may be of the same origin as ours. The similarity of our forms tends to prove it.

"Eventually metal domes were built, and the race prospered within. But our lives depend on their being kept in perfect repair. Machines were built which do practically all of the work in caring for our wants, and from the first we have adjusted our own gravity; to live normally under the gigantic pull of the new planet, which to you is Jupiter.

"Through the ages our lives became easier, and required less manual work. Machinery did everything we desired. Most of them were automatically repaired and serviced, while the permanent machines ran on through the ages without care. As generation after generation lived and died, under these conditions, we lost most of our former knowledge.

"When one of the atmospheric machines ceased to operate—we *could not repair it*! Instead, one of the other machines had to be speeded up, and the atmosphere pumped into the extra dome.

"At the height of our mechanical development this space ship was built. Then the race lost interest and were content to live in ease, without attempting to reach another planet. Three generations ago our people discovered the danger. Even our bodies had deteriorated until we *could not stand hard work*. The machines had begun to break down—we were headed for extinction!

"When I was a young man they succeeded in finishing the equipment on this ship. Three generations had been required to create enough fuel for only *two voyages*!

"I was selected as the man to explore the strange world, which we had been studying with the instruments of our ancestors. We had determined your exact mechanical development, and knew that you were capable of furnishing the engineers which meant life or death to our race.

"It is twenty years since I was left on the small island, and the ship returned to Jupiter. At that time we decided the date for this trip, to bring me back. In the meantime I traveled half way around the world in a small metal boat, before being picked up by a tramp steamer, as I dared not land near any civilized country. After I reached a settlement I had to learn your customs and language, and many other things about a completely alien people.

"I was furnished with an ample supply of gold, as we knew it was the metal that you valued highest. This purchased many things that would otherwise have been impossible to obtain, and also brought me a great deal of trouble. I was robbed of most of the wealth before I had been in civilization a year. The fact that a great deal was left on the small island is all that made my venture possible.

"I spent three years in an institution before they decided that I was a normal human being, and could take care of myself. I dared not tell them that I came from a different planet, or I would have failed in every way. I learned many things about the people of your world, but mainly that gold could buy almost anything.

"I lived for several years, by working at anything that I could obtain, trying to find someone who would finance an expedition to the island. No one would believe me when I said that I knew of a great fortune in gold. I finally found a man who *did* believe me, and he received one half of the gold as reward. It was not until then that I could begin the work that I started out to do, and nearly ten years had passed.

"I planned for several years before I dared try to obtain the people I needed. I studied everything I could about your engineering, and found that it was not of the same type as our own. For this reason I did not want a graduate engineer, as he would have to learn everything all over again in my cities.

"When I advertised for men, and told you of the wonderful mechanical development, it was the truth. I did mislead you to a small extent, in obtaining your promise to come with me, but the existence of my race depended on your work. My people will give you anything you desire if you will help them.

"When we left our cities, we didn't know whether we could even escape from the planet in this ship. There was no opportunity of testing it, until we started on the journey. Even the men at the controls had never handled it. All of their knowledge was obtained by years of practice, sitting in a stationary ship.

"When they left me on the island and returned to the planet, they *hoped* I could accomplish my purpose, but the chance of success was pitifully small.

"I have never enjoyed the comforts of other members of my race, but have spent my life in an alien universe, carrying around my big head; without friends or companionship. The gravity within our enclosed cities is lower than on your planet, making it easy for us to walk.

"After several years of study and planning, I knew there was only one way of accomplishing what I went after. It is the way I have done it. No one would have believed that I came from a strange planet; they would have thought me out of my mind. If I *had* persuaded them, I could have found no recruits for the work, no matter what I offered. I *know* how anyone feels about leaving their own planet, where they were born and brought up.

"You will find that the machines need work badly. Some of them are running only because we use several times the normal power to turn them. Our mining machines have not worked for more than a generation, and the mines remain idle. The metal supply is running short.

"The equipment which overcomes gravity, also furnishes us with power. When weights are lifted, with gravity almost eliminated, then allowed to sink with the full pull of Jupiter, it creates enormous amounts of energy for every use.

"It will be months before we reach our cities, and I hope that by that time you will feel satisfied with your forced migration. To my race, it was the only course which would avoid annihilation within a few generations.

"At first it will seem terrible to be shut in beneath a metal cover. But when you become accustomed to it, that feeling disappears. You depend just as much on a ship at sea or a plane in the air, but never think of it in the same way. We *must* trust you, as we will not know whether you are repairing or destroying our machines until we see the results.

"You will be given complete power and can draw upon my people for all of the help you need. You will be even more powerful than the rulers of the domes. My people decided that you deserved this position, long before we attempted to reach the earth and bring you back.

"I came to your country because the mechanical development is greater than in any other nation. You have greater love for engineering, and more of you are employed that way.

"I have told you everything about my home and my people, and leave it up to you as to the way you will act. We have only done what was necessary for the survival of our race, and hope that you will forgive us for stealing you from your own planet.

"You have complete freedom of the ship, to come and go as you please at any time. You are now considered part of our own population, and we both have the same interests. We hope you enjoy it."

For a moment Morquil gazed into the faces of the small gathering of people, then slowly walked from the room. There was complete silence, broken occasionally by a sigh as some thought of home exerted itself. An hour passed and they still had not moved. Each seemed to be waiting for one of the others to break the silence.

Finally Dick got to his feet. His words came slow, as if carefully weighed before using; the others listened intently.

"I know what each of you must be thinking; because I've been thinking the same thoughts. We are all in the same boat, without chance of leaving—headed for *Jupiter*! We have seen the last of the world where we were born. Either we take up our lives in this new existence, or die out here in space—destroying Morquil's race as well as ourselves.

"He says they can not survive without our aid. Our own world did not need us, or give us much for our efforts. If it had we would not be on this strange space ship. Morquil hired only people who were willing to leave their homes and friends—and we *applied* for the work. There really is not much that we can complain about.

"For one, I intend to do all that I can to make our future home the greatest civilization in the universe. Perhaps in the future years it will be possible for us to pay a short visit to our former planet. Perhaps our children will follow in our footsteps; enjoying greater honor, comfort, and luxury than they could possibly have had in our own world. I received little from my fellow men, and have *already* received more from Morquil than I ever had before."

As Dick sat down, John McCarthy's voice boomed out. "I'll follow Dick! He's the boss of this party, and if he's satisfied, I am. *Boy!* We sure do go places when we get started!"

The general laugh broke the tension, and each one spoke after a little hesitation. Each man slowly grasped the gigantic task that was facing them, and felt honored as a result.

It was a new world, farther advanced than their former habitation—which needed *them* to care for it. It was a big bite to chew—but they would do it!

Dick remained in his chair long after the others had gone to their cabins. His mind dwelled on the complete happiness and satisfaction that lighted Morquil's face, when informed of their decision. In that moment he was repaid for a lifetime in a strange world, amongst alien people. His return to Jupiter would be triumphal, with the earth people as his friends; come to save his race from extinction!

Barrow's mind wandered on, to the gigantic task that faced them. His would be the greatest responsibility, as head of all the domes. The other men would have a single city to care for. The thought of McCarthy as his assistant was comforting; he would be a great help.

The strange race of beings were putting every trust in the earthmen—putting themselves at the mercy of the seven strangers—and Dick knew the men would *earn* that faith!

He jumped when a hand touched his shoulder.

"Dick, won't you take your wife to her room—she feels sleepy!"

CHAPTER V.

Voyaging to Another World

DURING each waking period, Barrow spent many hours in the room with the miniature domes. They were beautiful models, which could be opened or moved as desired, by small levers on the foundation. Wires as fine as hairs were strung from one spot to another, while metal the size of thread represented heavy cables.

Slowly, an understanding of the strange civilization formed in Dick's mind, and he drew sectional maps of the location of all mechanical equipment. Other maps pictured the streets, so that it would be easy to reach any desired destination. When this was done, Morquil sent one of his men down to make as many copies as desired. Each engineer was to have a complete set.

The earthmen had learned to keep track of the time according to the system on the ship. Each "lix" included the time spent in sleep as well as one waking period. It was twenty-seven hours in length, but they all thought of it as a day.

Each lix was divided into thirty-six "migs." Each mig being just forty-five minutes in length. They were able to keep track of each mig, by their watches, although the time pieces were useless for any other purpose.

One lix, Dick returned the friendly smile of a member of the crew, and to his amazement the man spoke. "Chickiboo." For a moment Barrow was stumped, then realized that it must be a greeting.

When he was greeted the same way, by a second and then a third man, he tried to imitate the words. The man from Jupiter was so pleased that he almost danced, then spoke again. "Gootmording."

Dick's jaw almost dropped open; the man was trying to speak *English*!

Suddenly Barrow laughed. Morquil had been instructing his crew in the strange language, as well as telling them to greet the earthmen in their own tongue. He must speak about holding classes to learn the language. They would have to understand it, and the sooner they started the easier it would be.

The following lix, Dick stopped on the ramp to the machinery hold to listen. McCarthy was humming the tune of a song that had been the rage at home, but the words were "chicki-boo—chicki-boo—chicki-boo."

Barrow smiled as he approached, but the big Irishman didn't realize the reason. He was almost bursting with news.

"I've got it, Dick! I've found the key! Don't laugh, but I've discovered the working principle of this little machine, and it will lead to the secret of all others. In a month I'll know how this crate runs."

"Don't worry, I'm not laughing, John. I think it's great that you've got this far. I only wish the others would show as much interest. Not one of them has been down here for more than a few minutes, and they know little more than when we started."

"Aw! Don't take it that way, Dick. It isn't their fault. Didn't you ever see their *wives*? Those women won't let the men out of their sight for three minutes. Your wife and mine are different—they *trust* us! If we tell 'em the ship's okay, it's okay; but *them*—say, they can't tell their wives anything. The women in their families do *all* of the talking."

Dick laughed, but knew that it was close to the truth. The other men in the party *were* tied to their wives' apron strings. Aside from Dolores and Eileen McCarthy, none of the women trusted the space ship. They were afraid it might fly to pieces at any moment, although they had overcome their fear enough to find means of entertainment.

Small devices in the cabin showed miniature movies, with words in the tongue of the dome cities. Discovering this created desire to understand the language, and they eagerly attended the classes.

One lix Dick found Jerold Brown examining a piece of machinery. A few lix later Andrew Smith had joined him. Soon every earthman was spending his time in the machinery hold, with McCarthy acting as instructor. He would accept no excuse for being late at his classes—and they all arrived on time!

Weeks slipped by as the ship drove on through space. The earthmen learned to admire the men from Jupiter for their constant good-nature, although they were slightly childish.

The crew of engineers were slowly learning the rudiments of Jupiter's science. Barrow through his study of the domes, and McCarthy through study of the machines, far surpassed the others. At times both men spent hours in the model room, at others Dick examined the machines beside the Irishman. They compared notes until each knew the other's findings.

Dick took all the men into the model room once every third lix, and spent four hours instructing them in the civilization. Each man had his own set of maps, and marked down facts about his future location. Dick copied their notes on a large map, that covered all the cities. They used numbers to signify different mechanisms, to make it easier to describe equipment that was duplicated in more than one dome.

In a month they were able to carry on light conversation, and from then on mastery of the language was faster. The women far surpassed the men, due to desire for entertainment.

When he was able to question the crew, Dick received a terrible shock. *They knew less about the ship's operation than his own men!* They didn't understand their own equipment!

The people of the domes were content to enjoy the mechanical wonders of their ancestors—without bothering about how they ran. They used equipment for every purpose, without the slightest interest in why it worked. The earthmen suddenly realized what a gigantic task they faced. *Seven men*—to rebuild a civilization!

The men at the controls knew what reaction would take place by movement of a lever, but *didn't understand why*! Dick became slightly worried about reaching their destination—it was beyond all reason. Earthmen wouldn't have attempted to operate equipment they knew nothing about, by movement of controls to obtain the proper action.

It was no wonder these people had found it necessary to find engineers to run their machines!

Months slipped by as the ship moved steadily toward the giant planet. Every piece of equipment seemed to be the answer to perfection. This voyage had taught them more about mechanics than was covered in a complete engineering course on earth. It was of a far different kind, with gravity the basis of all operation. Even the space ship employed some of the same power, drawn from the nearest heavy body, then amplified until it reached enormous proportions.

Peter Yarbro was a practical chemist, and spent many hours trying to analyze the fuel. It was highly inflammable, yet could stand terrific compression without effect. When it was allowed to expand again, it reached the flash point immediately, creating enormous amounts of heavy gas. He believed it might be duplicated from crude oil, properly refined.

When Dick learned that there was a history of the space ship, in the metal books, his curiosity was aroused. He could read the language of the domes slightly, but not enough to study the intricate explanations. It was through these books that the dome men had learned to control the ship, and set the course for any desired planet.

Morquil's aid was enlisted, to translate the text, and he learned some amazing facts. A description of the fuel was given, but the base for manufacture was unknown, being of natural origin on Jupiter. As Morquil read farther and explained sections that Dick couldn't understand, the earthman felt uneasy.

The crew had abandoned all hope of returning to their home planet, the first time they started from the earth. They didn't understand what it meant to feel responsible for equipment. They manufactured enough fuel for two trips, according to the rating of consumption in the books—but Dick wondered?

The tanks were filled to capacity before the first trip, and hadn't been tested since. The happy dome people didn't consider that their ancestors might have been mistaken, or that actual operation might vary from the original plan.

For the first time in twenty years, the gauges were examined. Barrow and McCarthy crawled through the dust-coated passage beneath the floor of the machinery hold. They found a light switch, but the bulbs were so dust-coated that only a faint glow shed on the surrounding metal. They sneezed and coughed, as the dust-laden air filled their lungs.

"Darned if you don't get the craziest ideas, Dick. What good will it do to know how much 'ship juice' there is, anyway? We can't *make* it! This hole wasn't built for self-respecting men to crawl through."

"I don't know, John, but this trip may not be as easy as it appears. They've been driving at full force for months, when it seems to me that less power might carry us when we're not within the pull of some planet. I want to make *sure* that there's plenty of fuel. According to the books, the designers didn't expect the ship to be driven this hard."

John did a little cussing when they located the gauges, and found them so thick with grime that they had to be cleaned. He headed back through the dust for a cloth, with Dick's laugh following. "Alright, alright, but don't rub it in. Just because you happened to be in front of me, and there isn't room to pass, don't give you the right to laugh. Some day you'll be eating your share of dust, and will *I* laugh! I bet that the domes are *all* a mess."

Dick wrote down the reading of each gauge, as John cleaned the surfaces. He couldn't understand the strange numerals, and had to go over them with Morquil. Both men breathed a sigh of relief as they crawled back through the floor of the hold, and dropped the trap door in place.

An hour later Dick began to worry. According to Morquil, the tanks were *less than one-eighth full*. The big-headed man had gone over the figures twice, and was showing signs of agitation as he checked them again at Barrow's request. When he glanced up, Dick knew there was no mistake.

"The fuel *is* low Dick. According to the other trip, the greatest use of power is at the time we approach the planet, to fight the pull of gravity. Our trip from earth is only half completed, with the greatest need of fuel still ahead. You must think my race very stupid not to have thought of it?"

It took Dick a long time to answer. His mind was searching frantically for some solution. It was useless to ask help of the crew—they couldn't even *think* scientifically!

"No, Morquil. I don't think you're stupid, but I do consider your people very foolish. From the appearance of things *we will never reach the domes*!

"Unless something drastic is accomplished, the ship will smash to pieces on your planet. You don't know *anything* about the ship's operation, and we've only studied it for a short time."

They decided to inform the men immediately but say nothing to the women for the present. Within an hour of the discovery, Morquil warned the men at the controls to conserve the power as much as possible.

Every operation of the ship, was dependent on fuel. The generators for heat, light and controls, were turned by discharge through the tubes. At least *one* blast must be fired at *all times* to keep the controls sensitized, and develop power for emergency equipment. The other tubes were silenced.

During the rest migs Dick couldn't sleep, but spent every minute talking to John McCarthy. There *must* be some solution—*and they had to find it*!

CHAPTER VI.

An Engineer's Mettle

IN the morning the earthmen were called together. They came with smiling faces, which slowly changed to apprehension.

There were many suggestions in as many minutes, but none that gave a possibility of accomplishing the impossible. They had to stretch the fuel—*without visible means of stretching it*!

The women believed the meeting was a routine course in mechanics, and went on enjoying their entertainment. The men explained they were bothered by a knotty question about the machinery to account for their worried concentration. It would have been a terrible handicap if the women discovered the truth.

Three lix passed with little change. The fuel had been cut down for a while, but the ship didn't hold its course. Every tube had been fired to hold the direct route for Jupiter. They were constantly cutting into the meager supply that remained—*and had to overcome the deficiency*!

Due to the slight conservation of fuel the ship had been operating far below efficiency, and the cold of space began to seep through the walls. This affected the dome people more than the earthmen, and they suffered torture. Any change in temperature was unknown to them, they were chilled at a few degrees below normal heat.

Suddenly, during dinner on the third evening, Peter Yarbro jumped up from the table. The other men fastened eager eyes on his face, while the women watched in amazement.

He started to speak, then remembered the women, sat down quietly. "I—I think I've found the answer—to our *problem*! If you will join me in the hold, when we finish eating, I would like to talk it over with you."

Mrs. Yarbro was even more amazed. "Peter! I'm surprised at you. Jumping up from the table so excited, just because you happened to think of the answer to a *problem*! You ought to be ashamed."

In spite of his worries Dick lowered his head to hide the smile. If only Peter's wife knew what that problem was, she might not think it so strange.

Hardly a man touched his food, and as soon as they were out of earshot of the women, he spoke what was in his mind. The crew heard him at the table and many of them gathered to listen. For the first time in their lives they were worried. Their lives depended on the earthmen before they even *reached* their planet.

Yarbro hesitated. "I'm not so sure now, that I *have* found the answer. When it came to me, I thought it was simple, but now it seems more like a dream.

"Since knowing that the fuel was low I've racked my brain for something that might be used—and it had to be on the ship. Every *other* man was looking for a mechanical answer, and my efforts would be of little use. So I've searched for a chemical.

"*Water* is the only liquid in any quantity. I discarded it so many times that it left a headache, but my search always came back to the same place. It's the only thing we've got.

"All other liquids are in too small amounts, even if they could be used, and the ship is equipped only for chemical fuel—*in liquid form*!

"At dinner when I became so excited, I thought that water would do the trick. Now I don't know. It has oxygen in large amounts, which is vitally needed, but that's the only advantage.

"Even if we dared try, it might injure the tubes. Still I believe it's the only chance of salvation. It's the one substance on board, in any large quantity. What do you think?"

There wasn't a sound as the minutes passed. Each man searched frantically for the slightest hope; searched for the *one* chance in a thousand!

Dick finally broke the silence. "What is *your* plan, Peter? You must have thought of something?"

"No, that's just the trouble. I thought that water might mix with the fuel, even fire with it. It was only a brain storm I'm afraid."

After a moment Dick spoke again. "It *can't* be! Since there is no other substance—*we must use water*! There has to be a way—and *we've got to find it*! We might as well use up the water and die of thirst, as to drift around in space until we starve to death, or die in the dive at Jupiter."

Twice Mrs. Martin came down the ramp to take her husband to bed, but Dick sent her away. The men would stay there until they had found a solution—*they had to*! The fuel was fast disappearing!

Morquil still sat in the background. The other men from Jupiter had gone to their quarters. He could offer no suggestion, but listened carefully to every word they spoke. Finally he stood up.

"I hope that you can forgive me. In the last three lixs I have regretted that I ever saw your earth. It were better that my people die, than for us to carry people from a happy planet to die in space—because of our stupidity. We are no better than children without cares or worries. The men of the crew realized the risk, before they left the domes—but it is not your fault!"

"Aw, sit down you big-headed numbskull!" McCarthy's voice boomed out. "We don't blame *you*! We'll find some way to run this crate, and get there in one piece. You just made us go to work before we expected. Why! A problem like this is *simple* on earth—they'd solve it in *no* time! You just go to bed and stop worrying. We'll have everything fixed by morning."

Morquil's expression changed slightly, and he almost smiled. He started for the ramp as if taking the words literally, but half way up he faced the little gathering again. "Thank you, John. But I haven't forgotten that you were a famous liar in your home town—and you haven't lost your ability. Thank you anyway, you're very kind."

When McCarthy turned toward the others, he looked rather sheepish. But the forced smiles he received made him feel a lot better.

Hours passed, while each man told everything he had known about water. At last Dick stood up. "We've covered every possible reaction, and many that are seemingly impossible, but have overlooked one very vital point that will either help or hinder greatly.

"The fuel is subjected to terrific pressure. Naturally, any water that was used would receive the same treatment. In the compression chamber the pressure rises very fast, which must develop high temperature. The result is that we would not have water—*we'd have steam*! It would be almost *dry steam*!

"Water in the liquid form couldn't discharge oxygen fast enough to affect the fuel, but as steam it might. There is a good chance that steam may even *increase* the explosive power to a point that we can't even imagine. There's only one way to find out—*try it*!

"Every man here will admit that John has the most practical mechanical brain. It will be his job to find a means of injecting the water in the proper amounts. The rest of us can try to find any kinks in the system that he suggests. He knows every piece of equipment on board, and can pick whatever is best suited for the purpose."

As Dick sat down, John got to his feet. "This is one time that I'm ahead of you. While you've been talking I've been planning a way to do just that. There's an extra firing tube that can hold the pressure we want.

"Fuel for all the blasts is compressed in one chamber, then discharged through any desired tube. If we put the water under the pressure, with the hydraulic system, and let it seep into the chamber at a set rate—*it might work*! Valves can control the steam perfectly, and regulate the flow to whatever is desired.

"The tube will have to be shut off from the fuel tank every few hours, to be filled. Preheating the water will develop steam pressure, and it won't draw enough from the hydraulic system to affect the operation of the blasts.

"What do you say, shall we try it? It means shutting off all but the emergency tube for several hours, and it will be *cold*!"

Within five minutes they were hauling the heavy tube from the storage room. In an hour everything was ready to assemble, and each man knew exactly what work he was to do. A pipe line was run from the water tanks, to fill the steam chamber in position.

Dick was building an electric heating unit to encase the entire tube, which could be regulated for any desired temperature.

Half of the rest period had passed when the chamber was finished and they were ready to cut an opening in the compression unit. Perspiration poured down the body of every man, but not from the exertion. Each minute that passed ate deeper into the fuel. If water couldn't replace the liquid, they were helpless.

They wanted to install the tube, while the women were asleep. The ship would be too cold for comfort for a long time after the blasts could be started again. When the heating units in the hull were shut off it would become freezing inside.

Men raced through the ship, stopping at their staterooms on the way. Dick dropped three extra covers over Dolores without disturbing her, then slipped into the heaviest clothing that he owned.

Each man was occupied in his own room, in the same way. Heavy coats were taken to the men at the controls while the remainder of the crew were sent to a room with an emergency heating unit.

In fifteen minutes they were back at the compression chamber, and at the touch of a button the blasts were silenced from the control room.

By the time an opening was cut in the heavy tanks, the cold had begun to creep into the ship. The men worked desperately, and for a while perspiration dampened their clothing. Then the chill crept deeper—and they shivered. Their fingers grew numb, and they had to warm them over a small electric unit, but the opening slowly enlarged beneath their torches.

When the tube was fitted into the hole, and the metal began to flow around the edges, even the torches seemed to throw little heat. Dick knew his nose was frosted, and warned the others not to touch their nose or ears. According to John's watch it required three hours to fit the tube in place.

When they rang for the power to be turned on, they waited in vain. When minutes passed without reaction, they glanced at each other in consternation. Brown and Martin raced up the ramp while the others waited. Within a few minutes the tubes began to fire and warmth slowly drove back the numbing cold.

Water pipes had burst, and they hurried to stop the leaks. The main tanks were uninjured, as the cold hadn't penetrated the big supplies in storage.

Dick suddenly realized that Brown and Martin hadn't returned. When he reached the upper deck all of the women were gathered near the room where the crew had been left. The thermometer was only fifty degrees, even then, and they shivered in heavy coats.

Every dome man was stretched out on the floor! As Dick stepped within, his heart almost stopped beating—but they were only unconscious! His breath escaped in a long sigh, after holding it for almost a minute.

Brown and Martin were trying to revive the prone forms. The control men lay beside the others, brought there by the two earthmen. The eyes of first one then another, slowly opened, and they looked around in amazement. Cold affected them like an anaesthetic, causing complete unconsciousness.

When the ship reached normal warmth, they felt as good as ever. It hadn't been cold enough to freeze them, in their section, and not a man was injured. When they understood what happened, the men hurried back to the controls.

The heavy coils were soon fastened around the tube, and it was filled through a valve on the upper side. A gauge was set to register the pressure of the vapor within. They decided to raise steam pressure enough to equal the compression of the fuel.

It required fifteen minutes for the water to reach the boiling point, while they nervously held their watches. They could keep track of minutes and hours, although there was no longer day and night in their lives. According to their figures, they now ate dinner at three o'clock in the morning, and went to bed in the early afternoon.

They held their breath when the steam valve was opened. It moved slowly under Dick's fingers, while a thousand questions raced through every mind.

"Would it silence the blasts? Would it put them out of commission permanently? Was that moment, and the turning of that valve, the end of existence for them all?"

Dick glanced at the gauge on the tube, then jerked the valve shut. The pressure was still far below that of the fuel. He turned the heating unit on full, and watched the gauge climb higher. They didn't understand the numerals of the domed cities, but knew the pressure was getting terrifically high.

When he opened the valve again, the steam gauge *did not rise*! It held almost steady. The hiss of escaping steam, sounded through the heavy metal faintly.

The tubes began to fire spasmodically! Dick bit his lips, as he opened the valve a little wider. John McCarthy wiped the sweat from his forehead, as every face turned white as chalk.

They fired evenly again!!! The steam was working through the mixture—*discharging through the blasts*!

They felt their bodies sway under the effects of acceleration and exultance filled them. There was *some* reaction, at least!

Morquil appeared on the ramp, his face lighted by a smile. "*What have you done?* The ship is traveling at *almost twice the speed that it was before*! Is it all right?"

Dick sat down hard. Not a man in the crowd was able to answer. Success had left them speechless. Barrow was the first to recover his voice.

"Are you *sure*?"

"Yes, Dick! We took three separate observations, and each showed the same result—almost *double* normal speed! Does it mean what you wanted? *Can we reach the domes?*"

"I hope so, Morquil. If the steam has made *that* much difference, we'll get there without trouble. The water must be conserved as much as possible—and hope that it lasts. Whether it increases the power of the fuel, or simply creates an additional body to drive against, is not important. *We're getting there!*"

CHAPTER VII.

Jupiter and Trouble!

THE huge ship circled the planet twice, with the instruments adjusted to detect the metal of the domes. They spread over many miles of the surface, yet were like grains of sand on the enormous globe. When the gauges quivered over a section, hidden beneath the mists, every one breathed a sigh of relief.

It would be many hours before the ship was within the cities, but they were *home*! Every earthman had the same feeling. Jupiter was almost as much of a home to them as to the natives, even before they had seen it. They eagerly looked forward to sight of the domes that would be under their care.

John McCarthy entered the control room with a big tray of containers. "Here! It's not liquor, but I'll bet you enjoy it more. There's enough in each of these to *really* quench your thirst. I for one, will enjoy drinking all of the water I want, after five weeks on short rations."

It seemed impossible that the clouds outside could be deadly. They were beautiful in the reflected light of the sun, yet those vapors contained poison that no man could live in. The domes were the only place that life could exist on the strange planet.

As they dropped through the heavy mists, it created a feeling of dense fog. They could see nothing of the surroundings, trusting entirely on the instruments. It was like groping in the dark, yet the earthmen knew it had been done before, and the dome men showed no fear.

When a slight jar shook the ship, they breathed easier. *It had touched the ground!* They could feel some effect of the heavy gravity, even within the insulated hull. The ship slanted down at a steep angle, sliding forward with its own weight.

The earthmen didn't understand what was happening, but watched the actions of the dome men. They were using a different control board now, beneath the other panel. McCarthy was down in the hold, watching the action of machines that had been idle until now.

When they stopped, the mists disappeared from around them. Lights above outlined a huge metal passage. The ship started forward again and heavy doors slid back at the approach with bright light appearing beyond.

They were looking across sun-lit country; the most perfect scene they had ever witnessed. Strange trees, and growth of every description, spread in every direction. When the ship slid into the open, they were beneath one of the domes—enormous beyond their greatest imagination, and exquisitely beautiful.

While they watched spellbound, people started across the fields to greet the expedition. The women were well proportioned, and far different from the men of the race. Not as tall as the women of earth, or quite as well built, but their heads were much smaller than the men's.

All men were dressed in flowing robes, the women in much less clothing. They wore tight-fitting garments, like bathing suits of metallic cloth. They were happy and carefree, seemingly without a worry in their lives. Children came romping across the fields beside their parents.

Minutes, slipped by, and the people from earth hadn't moved. Sight of their new home was too wonderful to grasp at once. Instead of the gloomy metal covering they had expected, the curved surface above was finished in blue that resembled clear sky at home—as if they had reached the land of their dreams.

When their minds snapped back to reality, the dome men were being welcomed by friends and relatives. The babble of voices came faintly to the control room, from the power hull.

John McCarthy joined them. When the machines stopped, he came up to find the reason. Now the others watched as he gazed at the beautiful scene for the first time. Their own amazement was reflected in his eyes. When he looked up at the curved dome, his wife slipped her arm around him.

They were disturbed by the crew, returning with their friends to welcome the engineers. The dome people seemed completely happy. They were like children greeting their parents, holding the hands of the earth people and gazing into their faces with adoration. In their minds, the future was secure, and they no longer had a care in the world. Eileen McCarthy was so overwhelmed at the reception that she hugged two of the little women.

It was like a dream to walk across the heavy carpet of moss. There was no grass, but the velvet coat of green was quite similar. The trees were shaped like an inverted bowl, their branches conforming to the curve of the dome above. They were smaller than the trees of earth, with very large leaves.

The eyes of the earth people kept returning to the dome. It was hard to believe that it was not blue sky, except for giant supports that reached from the ground to the metal ceiling, hundreds of feet above.

When Peter Yarbro learned that he was in charge of this agricultural dome, his pleasure knew no bounds. His wife couldn't wait to see the home that had been prepared for them—and waiting almost twenty years.

A circle of buildings formed the foundation of the immense metal ceiling, as well as housing thousands of inhabitants. The back walls of the structures were always blank, toward the vapor beyond the miniature civilization. Each city was a world of its own, with a curved horizon at the top of the buildings.

In Yarbro's dome there were few means of travel, as every inch of soil was cultivated. The dome dwellers were past masters at farming, and loved this work more than any other type of labor. To them, it was a pleasure that vied with amusement machines of other cities.

When Mrs. Yarbro entered her new apartment, thirty stories above the ground, and stepped to one of the balconies, the view was superb. She was not interested in the next dome, but wanted to settle her own domain as soon as possible; completely happy.

The rest of the party entered an open car, mounted on a single track, and started for the next city. Every object that moved was operated by the control of gravity, and could develop enormous speed and power. It rolled swiftly across the open ground, to enter a tunnel three hundred feet wide, which carried all of the commerce between the cities. When it emerged in the next dome, the imitation sky was the same, but only a small portion of the ground surface was cultivated.

Small buildings dotted the level floor, which Morquil explained were the entrances of the mines, unworked for many years. Jerold Brown and his wife remained in this city, in an apartment as well situated as that of the Yarbro's, in the first dome.

Hours passed as they moved from city to city. When they reached the capitol, only the Barrows, McCarthys and Martins remained of the original fourteen. The others were in their own domes, settling down to the new existence.

Every occupation seemed to have been forgotten by the childish people, to come and welcome the beings from another planet. They lined every inch of the way, many deep.

The main dome was three times the size of the others. Supporting pillars, one hundred feet in diameter, seemed vague where they touched the ceiling above. Parks covered most of the ground, dotted here and there by amusement buildings and theaters.

Cars whizzed back and forth, as people gathered to see the strangers. For the first time in generations the amusement buildings were deserted. Since their arrival, Dick had seen no sign of work, and finally questioned Morquil.

"The people work one mig out of each lix, Dick. It is enough to carry on cultivation of the crops, and keep the amusement buildings running properly and efficiently."

Barrow was stunned. The working period would have to be increased to three immediately, then four and five. They seemed to think that bringing men from another world would do the work, and were apt to be disappointed when he started issuing orders.

When Dick and his wife were installed in their new home, and the McCarthys settled in a nearby apartment, Morquil hesitated. The Martins were anxious to see their own habitation, and looked at the dome man questioningly.

He finally spoke with hesitation. "I have bad news for you. The Martins will have to occupy an apartment in this city for a while. Their dome is out of order. Trouble developed soon after the ship left here, on this trip, and over a thousand people were killed. Every other city is overcrowded with refugees.

"It started with a strange banging on top of the dome, which kept increasing. No one knew what the trouble was or how to stop it, so they waited to see what happened. It didn't sound as if the ceiling was going to fall—but as if the banging came from *outside*! It was several migs before they knew the cause.

"When a large section crashed to the ground, it was a complete surprise, and caught the inhabitants unprepared. Soon the air was mixing with the poison gases from outside. People tried to escape, and most of them did. All except those that fell unconscious from the gas.

"Before the last of them reached the tunnel, green things dropped to the ground, and started after those who remained. They had to close the doors between the cities to keep the creatures from entering this dome. It is the first time that anything has happened to my people, and we don't know what it could be."

For a long time the earthmen remained silent. The troubles of this civilization had been dumped into their laps already—in the form of a terrible calamity. It sounded *almost* as if some kind of life forms had broken through the domes *from the outside*! Perhaps there was more danger than could be imagined. One dome had been injured, if not destroyed, and others might follow!

A meeting of the earthmen was called immediately, much to their surprise. Dick dared not let conditions stay as they were, for fear of future trouble. Action must be taken at once.

"We don't know what we're facing, but the fate of the race as well as our own lives, seem to be in danger. The break in the dome might have been accident, and the moving forms the imagination of fear. But we know that over a thousand people were killed—whatever caused the trouble!"

The men went back to their domes to rest, and plan some means of entering the deserted city, but were disturbed before they had time for sleep.

The agricultural dome had been attacked! The pounding had begun within a short time of their arrival.

One thing was certain, the injured dome had been *attacked*! It was not accident that the metal ceiling fell. *There were living beings in the gases outside their civilization!*

The first dome had been attacked just after the space ship left for the earth, and this attack came just after its return to the domes. There was little doubt that movement of the ship had disturbed the serenity of existence. Perhaps the gas creatures hadn't known what was beneath the metal hives until the ship appeared.

The banging on the agricultural dome, *had to be stopped*! A hole would let in the gas! Rifles, that had been brought back on the ship as curiosities, were given to each earthman. They loaded them carefully while they searched for some means of reaching the trouble.

When the leader of the dome heard what they were planning, he showed them sealed openings to a space between the sections of metal, which hadn't been used since the city was built. The dome was constructed in three layers, for insulation, and to give added protection. It was like a maze, to work their way toward the pounding through the network of struts. At times they had to crawl on their hands and knees, at others there were clearly defined passages.

They were afraid, and not ashamed to show it. They were hunting creatures which they knew nothing about—didn't even know whether bullets would affect them! They might face thinking beings, or forms of life that only wanted to search in the domes for food. It was not a pleasant thought.

Every rifle was cocked as they neared the source of the pounding. Every nerve drawn to the finest point.

Suddenly Dick stopped. He was ahead of the others and first to glimpse what they faced. He motioned to use the oxygen masks, as he fastened his own in place.

As they crept closer, light glinted on the giant pointed hammer, operated from beyond the outer layer of metal. It rose and fell at even intervals, through the rent in the upper surface. The ram had already crushed through two thicknesses of metal, and was battering at the inner layer.

The inside section was more like glass than metal and dim light passed through, but the outer layers were opaque. When the huge ram disappeared from the glow of light it left a gaping hole where it had been. It was of material they had never seen and glistened with a brownish hue. It appeared to shorten and expand in diameter, each time it struck the surface.

For a moment they hesitated, trying to decide the best means of attack. Whatever animated the ram was above their vision, and they had to be close to the opening to see it.

Each time the shiny object descended, the dome vibrated beneath their feet. As long as the vibration remained they were safe, but when it felt like a thud—the metal would be cracking!

Thousands of helpless people were depending on the action of earthmen, for their future existence. They seemed to think that it was only necessary to *tell* their troubles to these amazing strangers, to have them solved. Stories about the use of water to drive the space ship, had circulated throughout the cities, crediting the newcomers with superhuman powers.

As the little party crept nearer, they separated, to approach the opening from every direction. Dick was to fire first—if he saw anything to shoot at! It might be a powerful machine, clamped to the outer surface, instead of a being that could be injured. The glass globes of the masks were clouding with moisture, and it was hard to see.

A thud came, that didn't vibrate quite as much, and the men could feel the hair on their necks stiffen. It was now or never, and Dick fired although he was still several feet from the opening. He fired at the topmost section of the ram, hoping it might stop the hammering for a moment even if it didn't injure the equipment. Two more shots rang out, before the object could deliver another blow.

It was alive! The heavy ram *jumped* from the shock of the bullets, curving convulsively to one side of the opening. Then it drew back out of sight.

CHAPTER VIII.

Battle with a Monster

MINUTES passed, while the earthmen hardly dared breathe. Their ebbing heartbeat seemed to almost echo in their breasts. Then the object appeared at the opening, hesitated, and was thrust in!

The hammer was a head!!! It swayed back and forth, like the head of a huge caterpillar, and every gun fired in unison. Shot after shot pumped into the head with rapid and unerring accuracy.

The giant head moved from one side to the other, while two gigantic eyes peered around. It didn't know enough to draw back from the danger zone, but muscular reaction finally moved it out of sight.

Dick crept forward, motioning for the others to wait until he investigated. There was no need for all of them to enter the danger zone.

He turned the flashlight on, that had been strapped to his waist, and played it around the jagged opening, then climbed to the next level and searched again.

When he crawled to the outer surface, the creature was writhing a few feet away. He motioned, and the other men soon joined him, where they could watch the creature.

They were standing almost on the direct center of the dome, where it was almost flat. The flashlights penetrated the mists enough to mark out the shape of the attacker, when they were all centered.

Suddenly they felt sick to their stomachs.

It *was* a caterpillar! As loathsome a creature as they could have imagined with its curled body, and the farthest possible thing from a human being. A form of life that existed in the poison gases, where men would die within minutes. The muscles of the creature had to be terrifically strong, to move against the gravity of the huge globe.

Even at the center of the dome, they felt less effect of the neutralized gravity of the interior. It required effort to stand on their feet. Some effect of the neutralizers in the giant pillars, which eliminated most of the weight of the dome, enabled them to handle their bodies.

The creature before them was accustomed to normal gravity of the heavy planet, and even the metal of the dome was not beyond the pounding of its hammer. What they had mistaken for a battering ram, was the brown tip of the mammoth insect. From end to end it measured over sixty feet. The men finally turned away in disgust, as it writhed in muscular reaction.

John McCarthy was climbing into the opening behind the other men, when he happened to glance back. His flashlight dimly lighted the spot where the monster had been, and *it was gone*!

He hesitated with one foot in the air, then realized what had happened. The movement of the body had moved it farther and farther from the center of the dome. It had reached a place where the curve was sufficient to let it slide on the smooth metal. A moment later, a slight jar was felt through the entire structure—it had slid from the man-made mound, to crash on the ground below. Memory of that sight made a sober return to the interior.

Before they dared rest, metal sheets were carried to the opening and blocked in place. Then dome men welded them to the solid metal. They didn't want to see any of those creatures in the cities!

Twelve hours had passed by the time the opening was sealed, and the earthmen dragged their tired forms through the maze of supports for the last time.

They were almost asleep before they could reach their own apartments, and tumble onto comfortable beds. They had conquered the first problem.

Dick was awakened by an excited man, talking faster than he could understand the new language. When he grasped what the other was saying, he leaped from bed wide awake.

Every dome had been attacked!!! The caterpillars were pounding many spots on each one. They seemed to be trying to get at the creatures that had destroyed one of their number.

In that moment Dick felt like an old man. He thought of the space ship; the only way of attacking from the outside, and gave that up. There wasn't enough fuel to handle it, and the blasts might injure the metal domes. His mind searched frantically for some way of fighting *all* of the creatures—and knew it couldn't be done.

He was racing across the open ground, while thousands of people gazed at the banging overhead. Suddenly he stopped, then turned back toward his apartment, running just as hard. There was a system of communication between the domes—that *sometimes* worked! It was not efficient, but if he could get in touch with the others immediately, there was *one* chance!

He tried frantically to get a connection, but it wasn't until one of the natives helped with the intricate system of signals, that he heard the voice of Andrew Smith. A few moments later Philip Jones answered, then Jerold Brown and Peter Yarbro. Each man was given quick, yet explicit, instruction.

When Dick turned away from the phone, John McCarthy entered the room, followed by George Martin. The noise in the city had finally aroused them from their slumber.

John started to smile, but the expression on Barrow's face drove all thought of greeting away.

"*What is it?* I thought the people were doing a day's work—but *you*——!!!" His face turned ashen as he ran to the balcony, George Martin only a step behind. After gazing up for a moment, McCarthy turned slowly to face Dick.

"The worms? It sounds like *hundreds of them*! We better work fast, or they'll have the whole roof down around our ears."

"No, John. We can't fight them with guns. *They have attacked every dome on the planet!*"

When full realization came to the big Irishman, he sank slowly into a chair. "Then what? Have you got any plan—or are we helpless?"

"We've got work to do and plenty of it. There's a slight chance of saving the cities. I've already instructed the others."

As the three men raced toward the power plant, Dick explained. John and George were to do the work, while he traveled from dome to dome to make sure the people were prepared, and see that the power plants were used as he intended.

By the time they reached the entrance of the building, John nodded, and Barrow turned back as the other men entered the door. The first dome people that Dick saw were told to remove everyone from the buildings, and gather them in the open spaces of the parks. *Leaving no one within any structure!*

The expression on his face scared them even more than the pounding of the worms, and they hurried to obey.

Dick jumped into the nearest ground car. He couldn't be bothered traveling on the railroads. This happened to belong to the assistant head of the dome, whom he dispossessed. It jerked crazily across streets and parks, while he learned to handle the controls.

An hour later Dick was back at the powerhouse in the big dome. Every city was ready. In several places the hammering heads had broken through the outer layers, and were banging at the translucent inner ceiling. The creatures *had learned how* to break through.

The first worm that attacked, while the space ship was away, either took its time or didn't realize what was beneath the heavy metal. These creatures were working in earnest.

Heavy insulated cables ran from the powerhouse to the nearest metal pillars, where McCarthy and Martin were working desperately to fasten them in place. The booming voice of the Irishman had kept the natives back, although they crowded as close as they dared. They were really afraid, when the hammering grew plainer with each passing minute.

When the cables were fastened, John shouted to Dick, who was waiting in the powerhouse. He pulled a heavy switch, at the end of the wires.

The city was suddenly in complete darkness, then it flashed bright again as power flowed back into the thousands of coils in the ceiling material. Twice more it darkened, when the giant switch was thrown, and the lights came on again. This time it stayed bright.

Dick ran to the doorway, and gazed at the dome above. *It was silent!* The people were frightened, and moved restlessly about. Twice more he turned the power into the metal, and after one long darkened period, the city remained bright. *No sound came from the dome!* Either the worms were dead—or frightened away!

Within a week the doors to the deserted city were opened, and the earthmen passed through. When they glimpsed the interior, they stopped in consternation, then started to laugh.

Huge worms covered the ground, and smaller editions of the same species, crawled around them. *They were using the dome for a hatching place!*

They had only entered it to bring forth their young! It was not *brains* that tempted them to attack the city, but the instinct to find a protected place for their eggs. Since they had broken in, many of the young had hatched, and were crawling around the ground.

Sight of the earthmen seemed to excite their feelings, and several of the creatures started toward them. The men fired carefully, and the forms squirmed on the ground. The ones that came behind stopped, and some of the young tried to feed on the remains of their companions.

The sight was so sickening that the earthmen fired at every living thing they could see. Several of the wounded creatures crawled up the huge pillars, to disappear through the opening above, while the men shot at their disappearing forms. When the last caterpillar lay dead, the entire area appeared like a battlefield.

Three days later the gas had been expelled, and the hole in the dome repaired. The population was returning to their homes, burying the carcasses in the fields. The city was livable again, and they knew electric current would stop any future attack of the strange creatures.

Ten years later, Dick Barrow sat on the balcony before his apartment. His son John, eight years old, was playing with Dick McCarthy. While he watched the boys, his mind swung back to the earth the little group had left so many years before.

For three years they had talked of returning to their home planet, and the evening before the conversation reached a climax. They were starting in two months.

It no longer required years to manufacture fuel for one trip. All machinery was working at top efficiency, and they could turn out enough of the liquid in a month, to drive the ship back and forth several times. Crews of workmen had been trained to care for all mechanical equipment, and there was no longer need for the engineers from the earth.

The day the little party (it now consisted of eighteen with the four children), entered the space ship tears rolled down the cheeks of many of the crowd. The dome people had learned to almost worship these members of an alien race, and thought they would never leave. But when they realized that their leaders were dissatisfied, and wanted to return to their native planet, they aided in every way they knew how.

The ship was out of port for less than a week when the people became restless. They hardly spoke, even at meal time, and for the first time in ten years there were petty quarrels.

When Barrow called them to the main cabin, they came grudgingly, then slowly the expressions changed. Smiles appeared on their faces, and their heads moved with sheepish nods of assent.

"We're fools, and you all know it. We were happy in the domes, happier than we ever were in our lives before. We didn't appreciate it and longed to return to the earth. We wanted to leave, yet had everything there to live for. We had comfort, every pleasure, and more friends than we can possibly have on our own world. *I feel ashamed!*

"Right now we *wish* that we were back in our own apartments, and might as well admit it. The earth is not what we want, *we want the domes*! They are *home*!!!

"The best thing for us to do, now that we are on the way to the earth, is establish commerce.

"We can create friendship between the planets, but we are natives of Jupiter! Our interests will always be with the dome people. We have almost become part of that race, and they have given us everything in return. They even gave us our freedom when we wanted it. *We belong there!*"

Ten years more passed, and John Barrow was beginning to help with his father's work. Vacationing in Jupiter's domes had become so popular on the earth that they were building another city to accommodate the tourist trade. It was the third to be added to the original six. Merchant ships were constantly discharging goods from the earth, and carrying back rare metals.

Space ships from the earth, designed after the original Jupiter ship, were searching the little known planets for minerals. Domes were being built on three of the smaller globes, and pioneering humans migrated to new worlds. There was danger, yes, but also fame and fortune for the hardy people who would inhabit them.

The earth had changed a lot, since the visit of the space ship. They had adopted the principle of controlling gravity, and tremendous structures were the result. New buildings were several times as large as the greatest structure of ten years before. Both planets had benefited from the friendship, and both were happier as a result.

As Dick Barrow's mind ran over these facts, he smiled and spoke aloud to himself. "And all of this in twenty years—it seems incredible!"

"What did you say, dear?" asked Dolores.

Dick smiled as he glanced at her. "It's nothing. I was just thinking. Remember the night you fell in front of my table in the hotel? And I thought it was *accidental*—you scheming gold-digger!"

The ruler of the domes ducked when his wife threw her book—but she didn't throw it very hard.

THE END